"BUD"

Bud's Flatboat Adventure

WRITTEN BY CALLIE SMITH

ILLUSTRATED BY R. CAROL SKINNER

FOR

my grandparents,

who first delighted me with stories of the past,

AND FOR

Ken, who brings all stories to life

ISBN/SAN 0-9703951-1-6
The display and text type are set in ITC Stone Serif.
Printed in Mexico

First edition, August 2003

ABOUT THE AUTHOR

Callie Smith was born in Noblesville, Indiana, in 1978. She received her B.A. in English Literature from Ball State University and has been an historic interpreter at Conner Prairie since 1996. *Bud's Prairietown Holiday* is her first work of children's fiction.

ABOUT THE ILLUSTRATOR

R. Carol Skinner has worked as a freelance artist and illustrator from her Carmel, Indiana, studio for the past 25 years. Her interest in both drawing and composition has strengthened her art, and she has worked extensively in both pen & ink and watercolor. Illustrating books has always been a dream of the artist, and she looks forward to much more.

TABLE OF CONTENTS

AUTHOR'S NOTE

Bud's adventures take place in the year 1836. Some of the objects, words, and phrases he knew about may not be familiar nowadays. That's why certain words in this book are set in *italic* print. Bud and his friends try to make the meanings of the words clear. However, if you'd like to know more, these words are explained further in the "Glossary" at the end of the book.

CHAPTER ONE Duty and Delight

"But I want to go."

"You can't."

"Why not?"

"Because."

Bud opened one eye. He'd been napping on the doctor's porch. The late afternoon sun shone over the grove at the edge of Prairietown. Its rays warmed his fluffy yellow fur against the chilly air. What more could a cat want? It was a perfect March day. It was perfect, that is, until Elizabeth Bucher came storming out of the doctor's kitchen.

"You're as bad as Ma!" she yelled and dropped herself onto the edge of the porch.

The floorboards bounced underneath Bud's head. He jumped up and ruffled his fur, but Elizabeth didn't even see him. She was busy frowning and wiping a tear from her eye. Bud forgot about his nap. He walked over and rubbed against her arm. She picked him up and hugged him. He felt her heart beating quickly under her brown woolen shawl.

"It isn't fair!" she yelled.

"Life isn't fair, Elizabeth." Elizabeth's older sister, Abigail, stood inside Dr. Campbell's kitchen door. "Now come inside. We're lettin' a draft into the house with this open door."

Elizabeth sighed. She stood up with Bud and carried him into the kitchen.

"Now, Elizabeth, don't bring Bud inside! What'll Mrs. Campbell say?"

"He wants to get warm, too, Abby." Elizabeth took Bud to the chair between the kitchen table and the *woodbox*. They sat down. "You said there were mouse droppings in the pantry yesterday. He can mouse for you. Besides, Mrs. Campbell won't know."

Abigail shook her head, but she closed the kitchen door. Elizabeth let Bud down to the ground. The pads of his paws met the warm floorboards. How nice that felt! He went over and sat on the stone hearth. He kept his tail just far enough from the cook stove that it wouldn't brush the stove's hot iron legs. Still, he could feel its heat all along his back.

"I don't see why I shouldn't ride the flatboat with 'em to New Orleans. Andrew invited me. He said I could start by comin' along tonight and helpin' 'em load the boat. They're gonna be startin' any minute now, and I want to go."

"So that's it."

"What's it?"

"The only reason you want to go help load the flat boat tonight," began Abigail, grinning, "is because Martin Zimmerman's gonna be helpin' load the boat, too."

"What do you mean?"

"I mean you and Martin Zimmerman have been thick as thieves lately. I wouldn't be surprised if one o' these days he talked to Jacob about callin' on us at home and courtin' you."

"He would not! You take that back, Abigail Bucher! You're the one that's of a courtin' age, not me."

Abigail grinned again and stood up. "So?" she asked, grabbing a pair of brownish-green *kettle holders* from the mantel.

Bud looked from Abigail to Elizabeth. The girl was frowning.

"I don't care a lick about loadin' the flat boat tonight," said Elizabeth, trying to ignore her sister's grin. "I want to go with them tomorrow! Just think, Abby! I'd be seein' a city! We've never seen one before! We've never even seen a big town like Indianapolis. How delightful! I'd bring back so many stories!"

"Elizabeth, Andrew McClure invited you. His father didn't."

"But our brother owns part of the boat, too. In fact, two of our brothers are makin' the trip."

"Yes, and they didn't invite you, either." Abigail used the kettle holders to lift a steaming iron kettle from the stovetop. "Jacob wants to sell as many of our things as possible in New Orleans. That's why he's takin' along a strong boy like Ethan. The two of 'em will be able to do all the loading and work. That's part of how they support our family. If there were extra space on the boat they'd take more maple sugar or bring another calf. They wouldn't just bring someone along to gawk at the city."

"I wouldn't be just someone to gawk at the city!" Elizabeth tugged at her shawl, bringing it closer around her. "I'd help with the boat, same as Ethan and Andrew."

Abigail poured steaming water into the bowls on the dry sink. She was shaking her head. She returned the kettle to the stove and said:

"Ethan can lift twice as much as you can, Elizabeth. Andrew will be helping load the barrels and steer the boat, too. They only need five people. Andrew and Ethan both have to learn how the flatboat works. They'll be the men taking their own goods down river some day. That'll be part of makin' a livin' and supportin' a family. But *you* . . ."

Bud perked up his ears. He heard footsteps in the next room.

"Abigail!"

It was Mrs. Campbell's voice! Abigail glared down at Bud. She took a step toward him, but he leapt to his feet and scampered to the pantry. He got there just in time, for he heard Mrs. Campbell walk into the kitchen.

"Abigail," said Mrs. Campbell's voice, "we'll take our tea now."

"Yes, ma'am. Green or store tea?"

"Store tea will be fine."

"Yes, ma'am."

Mrs. Campbell's footsteps left the kitchen and disappeared further into the house. Bud relaxed. Only then did he smell the pantry scents all around him. He looked up.

The walls were lined with shelves. They were full of jugs and crocks. Some crocks had lids. Some were covered with squares of linen and tied up with string. Some were empty and turned upside down. Catsups, vinegars, preserves, dried fruits and vegetables, vegetables packed in sand—the Campbells had been using their winter supplies for months now. It was still March, though. Fresh greens and fruits wouldn't be growing for a good while yet. Of course Abigail would be worried about a mouse getting into the final, precious servings of the winter's food.

Bud sniffed one of the larger crocks sitting on the floor. Was that beef? Its scent was very faint. It must have been packed in salt. Hmm . . . perhaps Mrs. Campbell *did* have reason to be worried about a cat in the kitchen! That beef would have tasted awfully good just then.

"It's just not fair," he heard Elizabeth say again.

Bud went back to the pantry door and looked out.

Abigail had a knife in one hand and a block of lye soap in the other. She shaved off bits of soap into her steaming dishwater. A blue and white teapot sat on the kitchen table near Elizabeth's elbow. Steam rose from the spout. A faint scent of tea already filled the air. Elizabeth, however, was slouched down in her chair, frowning. Abigail must have seen her sister's frown, too, when she turned around. She set her knife down and spoke:

"Andrew's learnin' to help his family the best he can. We all need to learn to do that. For Andrew, that means workin' a flatboat in the spring. For you, that means workin' with Ma to boil up the last of the sap for maple sugar. It means practicin' your stitchin' so you can sew dresses as fine and as sturdy as Ma sews 'em. Besides, didn't she promise to take this time before plantin' to work with you on makin' your piecrusts softer and flakier? The men folk won't be home until April. Imagine how much time that'd take out of your work if you went with 'em."

"It takes time out of their work, too."

"It *is* their work."

"Then the men folk have the better work. Boys shouldn't get to have all the fun."

Elizabeth didn't even look up. Bud went over and rubbed against her woolen stockings, which showed from beneath the hem of her dress. He *knew* Elizabeth would enjoy ending the winter with her mother's lessons. Just the other day he'd heard Martin Zimmerman say Elizabeth's pies were almost as good as his mother's. Martin loved pies, and that was quite a compliment!

Abigail joined Bud at Elizabeth's chair. She squatted down and scratched between Bud's shoulder blades. Then she looked up into Elizabeth's eyes.

"We each have duties. Don't you want to do yours and help the family the best you can?"

"You don't understand," Elizabeth sniffled. "You get to come to town every day to work with Dr. Campbell's fancy rooms and dishes. Why should you care about seein' anything else?"

"Do you think that's why I come to work for Dr. Campbell?"

Elizabeth wasn't listening to her sister. "You don't understand 'cause you don't have to care about seein' anything else besides what you see every day. But I do!"

Abigail was silent. Elizabeth sniffled again. Then she stood up and ran to the door. Bud had to squat down on the floor to avoid her feet. She flung the door open and ran down the porch stairs. Bud looked at the door. Should he follow her? He looked back at the pantry. He hadn't smelled a mouse in there today. He looked up at Abigail. She was at the door, looking out after her sister. The girl wore a hurt look on her face. No, Abigail wasn't worried about the mouse just then, either.

Bud darted past Abigail's feet and onto the porch. The chilly air met his face as he ran down the steps. He leapt up and over the back gate and followed Elizabeth down the road into town.

CHAPTER TWO
A Curious Load

River Road was still muddy from the morning's rain. Bud felt his paws sliding beneath him. There was Elizabeth, running down the road ahead of him. As she passed Mr. Whitaker's store she almost tumbled over Martin Zimmerman, who was coming down the porch steps.

"Whoa there!" Martin laughed. Then he saw Elizabeth's face. "What's wrong?"

"Nothing," she answered, blushing. She hurried on past him.

"But what . . . ?"

"Nothing!" she yelled over her shoulder before Martin could finish.

He stared after her. Bud sat down in the road and did the same. Elizabeth ran until she came to Curtis' tall, white-washed house and knocked on the door. It opened, and she went in.

Bud looked up at Martin. The boy was staring at the Curtis door with a hurt look on his face. "Now what's got her goat?" he asked under his breath.

Bud rubbed his head against the boy's leg. He was sure Elizabeth hadn't meant to be rude.

Martin looked down at Bud.

"There's no talkin' to her when she's like that, Bud," he said, squatting down to scratch Bud's ears. "I hope she's all right."

Bud rubbed his nose in the boy's hand. Elizabeth and Jenny Curtis were good friends. Elizabeth would at least have *someone* to comfort her.

"Weren't you gettin' Jacob for us?" asked a voice loudly from inside the store.

"I'm goin'!" Martin yelled back.

He gave Bud one last scratch. Then he stood and walked up the road, leaving Bud to sit in the mud.

Bud could still hear muffled voices behind him in Mr. Whitaker's store. He cocked back his ears. He couldn't quite tell what they were saying. A horse shuffled and neighed nearby, too. He wasn't ready, however, for the sharp noise that suddenly came:

WHAM!

Bud leapt into the air and scurried behind an old oak tree.

"Get hold of it, Andrew!"

"I have it!"

Bud craned his neck around the side of the tree. James Whitaker and Andrew McClure were trying to lift a wooden barrel from the store's back porch.

WHAM!

They dropped it onto the long, flat bed of a sledge sitting below on the ground nearby.

"Just one more, my boy!"

"Yes, Sir."

Andrew followed Mr. Whitaker into the back room of the store. Bud crept out from behind the tree. What were they loading so late in the day? He tried to get a good look.

Mr. Whitaker came back out onto the porch.

"Good o' your pa to invite me along on the trip," he said. "People are all boilin' up *country sugar* this time o' year. My father and I get so much of it in trade that we're glad for the chance to get it to market!"

"Yes, Sir," said Andrew, almost out of breath with lifting his end of the barrel. "Pa wants to get goin' good and early tomorrow."

"Gotta go early to get the best prices."

"Are we ready?" yelled a voice from the road.

Bud glanced around the other side of the tree. Jacob Bucher, Daniel McClure, and Martin Zimmerman were walking towards them. They wore their heavy overshirts, and each of the first two men carried a rifle at his side. Mr. Bucher had a knit cap pulled down over his ears.

WHAM!

Andrew and Mr. Whitaker dropped the last barrel onto the sledge.

"Ready!"

"Let's hook up the horse and get down there," said Mr. Bucher.

Mr. McClure brought the horse from the other side of the store. When they'd hitched it to the sledge, Mr. McClure mounted the horse and guided it out onto the road. Mr. Bucher and Martin Zimmerman followed close behind. Several cotton pokes sat on the store porch. Andrew grabbed their drawstrings and ran after the group.

Bud stepped out from behind the tree. Abigail had spoken of the men loading barrels for the flatboat trip. Were these the barrels? Something about this trip had excited Elizabeth. Now Bud was curious, too. He could at least catch a glimpse of what the men were doing. So when they went south, Bud followed.

When they came to the end of River Road, Mr. McClure turned the horse onto a path down the hill. It was the way to the river. Bud came this way often in the warm weather. When the banks of the river were cool under the shade trees, he'd nap there or watch for chipmunks and rabbits that came down with the same idea.

Trees became thick around the group as they went down the path. Every now and then, they could see bits of the White River beyond the trees. Its water glowed orange as it reflected the setting sun. The sledge went to the bottom of the hill and further into the woods beneath. Andrew, Martin, and Mr. Bucher followed it. Bud followed them.

His ears became accustomed to the sound of the horse's breathing and the sledge blades scraping along the ground. Eventually, another sound came to his ears. It was the soft, slow sound of the river. The men must have heard it, too, for they slowed their pace.

When the sledge reached the river bank, Bud hung back. He stepped behind a fallen tree and raised his eyes over it. There, near the edge of the river, floated a boat. It must have been as long as a cabin! Several ropes tied it to trees on the riverbank. It rose and sank gently with the movement of the water. The water was high from the rain and the melting of the winter's ice. This was what the men had been waiting for. He'd heard them talking about it at the store for weeks now. They were guessing among themselves as to when the water would be high enough to carry their flatboat. Bud had never been exactly sure why high water was so important, so he was all the more interested in what the men were doing tonight.

WHAM!

Bud dropped down to the ground.

"Be careful with those barrels!"

"Yes, Pa!"

Bud crawled to one end of the tree and peeked around the edge. The men were taking crates, barrels, and *hogsheads* one at a time onto the boat. It would surely take them forever to fill its huge space! Bud had been down to the river in past springs to watch the men as they built their flatboats. But he'd never seen a finished boat being loaded. What work!

The men pushed their pieces of cargo under the flat-roofed enclosure that covered most of the deck. Mr. McClure was very particular about how they arranged the goods. He had the others moving the containers and fitting them into tight spaces here and there.

Bud yawned. The ground near the base of the tree was pleasantly warm. He laid his chin down on his paws. When wheels and the hoof beats of another horse approached, he turned his head. Mr. Curtis rode up with a wagon full of barrels and sacks of his own. Would they load those onto the boat, too? The men had sure set a big task for themselves for this late at night. Bud yawned again and closed his eyes . . .

A spider crawled across his ear. Bud woke up and pawed it off. He listened. All seemed quiet. He opened his eyes and searched the riverbank. The horses, the sledge, the wagon—they were all gone. And the men? Leaves rustled from time to time down by the bank. Bud thought he could see the outline of a man there, sitting with his back against a tree. Was that Mr. Bucher's knit hat? Bud waited.

Eventually, the leaves stopped rustling. Bud came out from behind the tree to look around. Everything was dark except the river. It seemed to soak in the moon's rays and glow with a fuzzy blue light. Bud made his way down there, closer to the river's edge.

The bank was clear of barrels. Everything must have been loaded. Would there have been any room for Elizabeth, after all? Bud placed his front paws upon one of the ropes going out to the boat. It creaked and swayed.

"Is someone there?"

Bud froze. He saw eyes peer out from over the edge of the boat. . . then a nose . . . it was Andrew!

"Bud?!"

Leaves rustled in the distance. The two of them stopped. They waited quietly.

"Bud," whispered Andrew after another moment. "Come here, fella. Just don't let Mr. Bucher see you." He reached his arms out along the length of the rope. "Come out on the rope a little. I'll get you."

Bud tried the rope again with his front paws. He jumped. His back feet had hardly touched the rope before he was running along it towards the boat. He might lose his balance if he slowed down!

"Gotcha!"

Bud felt himself lifted over the edge of the boat. Andrew brought him down into a woolen blanket on the floor. Bud had meant to look around and explore the boat. The blanket, however, made him pause. It smelled of corn shuck ticks and wood smoke—two things that meant a warm night's rest. Bud drew his tail up around him. Andrew brought the blanket up around them both. Soon they were asleep.

CHAPTER THREE
The Accidental Passenger

"Oink, oink!, OI-I-I-I-NK!"

"Go on!"

CRACK! Wood slapped against wood.

Bud shot up out of Andrew's blanket.

Stamp. Stamp. Stamp.

Someone was coming onto the boat! Bud grabbed the nearest wooden crate with his claws. He crawled frantically to the top.

"Bud, wait!"

The boat's roof curved upward in the center. There was just enough room left between it and the barrels for Bud to scrunch himself between them.

"Come back, Bud!"

He felt Andrew trying to pull him out from his cramped space. Bud dug his claws deeper into the wood. He would not be moved.

"Oi-i-i-i-nk!"

The flatboat swayed in the water. Hoofs beat quickly across the boat's floor. Bud moved further back under the roof and hid himself in the shadows.

"Git!" came Mr. McClure's voice.

"Go!" shouted Mr. Bucher.

Bud turned around. He could just barely see out from underneath the roof. The men had dropped a wooden plank between the bank and the side of the flatboat. It made a bridge. They were now herding and coaxing a group of hogs aboard!

"Oi-i-i-i-nk!"

"Moo! MOO!" came other, low-pitched voices.

Bud cocked his ears forward to listen better. Were those calves?

"Mornin', sleepy-head," said Mr. McClure to his son.

Stamp. Stamp. Stamp.

Step. Step. Step.

"Mornin', Pa. Can you . . . ?"

"Just a minute, Andrew. Is everyone on?"

"Yup."

"All aboard!"

"Ready!" Several voices yelled together.

Bud could see Mr. McClure's legs. The man stood just above the hogs on the *gunnel* of the boat. From there, he stepped up onto the top of the roof. Bud heard the other men doing the same.

"Come on up, Andrew."

"But wait! Bud . . ."

"Andrew, you just watch as we start out. You can lend a hand later."

"But Pa . . . "

"Ready for the ropes! Andrew, stay back."

Bud crawled over the tops of the crates and barrels until he came to a crack between two of the boards. He saw the river bank. It was getting further away!

"Are we far enough out?"

"Yup," replied someone else.

Was that Mr. Curtis' hired man, Matthew Whitesman? Bud thought he recognized the voice.

"All right."

That was James Whitaker!

The boat seemed to pause. Good! They were not going any further away from the bank. Bud wrapped his tail around him. He continued to watch out the crack. Maybe this was all the further they were going. Yet . . . he put his eye closer to the crack. The bank was moving again! No, it must be the boat moving. They were going down river!

"It'll be all right, Bud," Andrew whispered. He was hanging his head upside down from on top of the roof.

Bud was not sure what to think. They were floating south. He recognized the different parts of the riverbank they passed. He strolled along those parts of the bank some days. Mice, rabbits, all sorts of little animals would come down to the river. But . . . no. Bud did not recognize this next part of the bank. He had never been this far south along the river!

The hogs oinked more quietly now. Bud could hear the men talking above him. He relaxed a little and looked around. A hogshead was beneath him. He lowered his head to sniff. It smelled like . . . tobacco? Yuk! Bud hated that smell. He sniffed some of the other barrels and crates. Oats, flour, pork, bacon, ham, vinegar, raccoon skins—there was so much to smell!

But wait! All of that was going to New Orleans. Wasn't that what Elizabeth had said? Was Bud going to New Orleans? He crept to one end of the boat where the roof above him ended. There were the hogs and calves beneath him on the deck. He crawled to the other end of the boat. It opened over the water! He crawled back to the middle. He was going to New Orleans. He had no way of getting off the boat. He'd have to . . .

Was that a scratching noise? Bud looked beneath him. Nothing. He waited. There it was again! He breathed very, very quietly. Even his whiskers remained still. Yes, something scratched against the wood nearby. Ten minutes must have passed. He kept waiting. Finally, a tiny, pink nose appeared over the edge of a barrel. Whiskers followed. They bobbed up and down beside it. Then the mouse they belonged to raised itself to the top of the barrel!

Slap!

Bud brought his paws down on the mouse's tail. He didn't have a good grip, though. The little varmint slipped out of his grasp. Bud leapt again. Again, the mouse slipped away. Bud chased after it, back and forth in the narrow spaces beneath the roof. He knocked the barrels together with the weight of his leaping. The barrels might have fallen over if they hadn't been

stacked so close together!

"What's goin' on down there?" asked one of the men from above.

Slap!

Bud just barely caught the mouse's tail. It slipped out of his paws, again. He had to catch that little varmint before it ate its way into any of the barrels!

"What the . . . ?" came another voice from above.

The mouse darted out from underneath the roof and onto the *gunnel*. Bud threw himself out after it and . . . got it! He reached down and clenched the mouse's tail between his teeth.

Moo!

Bud looked up as the mouse dangled from his mouth. He was staring right into the eyes of a huge brown calf!

Moo!

The hair on his back and tail stood on end. Bud leapt straight up into the air and landed on the roof of the flatboat.

"A cat!"

He twisted around. There were the flatboat men, staring at him. And there was Andrew, wide-eyed and silent. Bud bit the mouse's tail tighter in his mouth.

"Bud?"

"Naw . . ."

"Yeah, it's Bud!" said Mr. Whitesman, taking the clay pipe out of his mouth.

Most of the men stared at Bud in surprise. An angry look, however, passed across Mr. McClure's face.

All of Abigail's words with Elizabeth came back to Bud's mind. Like Elizabeth Bucher, he hadn't been invited. He was an extra passenger. He couldn't help the men guide the boat. He wasn't worth any extra money to them at market. No wonder Mr. McClure looked so angry!

Mr. McClure moved towards Bud. Bud had no where to go. He sat, frozen under Mr. McClure's scowl.

CHAPTER FOUR
A Close Call

"Darn varmint!"

Mr. McClure raised his hand and brought it down at Bud. Bud flinched. Mr. McClure, however, didn't touch Bud. Instead, he snatched the mouse out of Bud's mouth. He turned to the side of the boat and flung the little thing overboard. "Go find yer own food!"

The mouse made a little splash in the water near the shore. Everyone watched as it dragged itself out of the water and scurried into the brush a few feet from the river's edge.

"Good riddance!"

Bud stared at the shore. He was still shaking from the fear that Mr. McClure meant to snatch *him* up and fling *him* overboard!

"That's a good mouser," said Mr. McClure. He picked Bud up and scratched him behind the ears.

Pur-r-r-r.

"Good Bud," said Andrew, too. He came up beside his father and patted Bud's back.

Mr. Whitesman laughed. "Some folk say black snakes are best for eatin' up all yer varmints . . . ," he reached over and scratched Bud's chin, ". . . but I'd take this fella any day."

"So you decided to come along, did you?" asked Mr. McClure. He gave Bud one last scratch between the ears before setting him down. Mr. McClure went over to help Mr. Whitaker at one of the *sweeps*. Mr. Whitesman joined Ethan Bucher at the other. Bud stayed at Andrew's feet. The two of them watched the men at their work.

By now, the sun was high in the middle of the sky. Bud felt its warmth on his fur even through the chilly breeze. No wonder the river was so high these days! Ice couldn't help but melt under a sun like this.

Bud looked back at the men. They wore their felt hats pulled close over their eyes. The hat brims threw half of their faces into shadows. Two men stood on either side of the flatboat roof. It would often take two of them, Bud supposed, to control one of those sweeps. The sweep handles were a good size, after all. They were the trunks of young trees!

Bud turned around to face down river. He sat at the edge of the roof on its warm, curving planks. Below on the deck, the hogs and calves wandered about. Beyond them and beyond the square front of the boat, flowed the White River. The boat floated down stream, first towards this side of the river, then towards the other. The men kept it away from the shores and banks, and so they floated through the water smoothly enough. Trees of all different shapes and sizes lined the edges of the river. They reached their bare branches out over the water. Every now and then, sparrows or a blue jay would dart out from the woods and fly above them. Bud even saw the fat, red chests of the robins newly-arrived for spring!

"Is that the old grist mill?" asked Ethan, pointing at a huge building on the slope of the river's left bank. "It's about mid-day. We must be gettin' on towards Indianapolis by now."

"That's right. There's the National Road bridge beyond it," added Mr. McClure.

The man motioned for Andrew to come to his side. He put his hand on his son's head as he pointed to the outline of a bridge stretching across the water in the distance. The boy smiled. Bud could see why Elizabeth got so anxious to go on the trip. Andrew's whole face seemed to light up at this new sight. Elizabeth probably got excited, herself, listening to Andrew talk about all the new things he'd see and do.

On they went, down river. It must have been shortly after the boat passed under the bridge that Bud's eyes drifted shut. He wasn't sure how long his eyes had been closed when a noise suddenly made him jump up, wide awake, with his tail puffed out in fear. He looked around him quickly. It was only Mr. McClure laughing! Bud could tell by the other men's faces that he wasn't the only one surprised by the laughter. He relaxed a little.

"Now, look," said Mr. McClure, still laughing but pulling his son closer. "Now look down here. See those *shallows* comin' up? We're comin' on Hog Island now."

Bud looked out ahead of the boat. At a certain point, the water seemed to be a lighter color. Its waves there became shorter. They rippled more.

"Hog Island?" repeated Mr. Whitesman, not seeming to know what it was.

"That's right," said Mr. McClure. "You didn't get out here till '33, did you, Whitesman?"

"No."

"Well, I was livin' near here at Fall Creek back in '31," began Mr. McClure. "Andrew here was too young to remember, I expect. A fella tried to get a small steamer up the White River to Indianapolis."

"No!"

"Yup. It was in April, when the river was already down from what it was in March. Folk was welcomin' the steamer in. Tradesmen were probably thinkin' they were gonna make Indianapolis the next Cincinnati or Louisville. Thought they were gonna bring all the steamboats through town with their goods from the east. Oh, I'm sure they had all sorts o' ideas."

"Oh no."

"Oh yeah! So along comes General Hanna with his steamboat. You know steamboats need a river all along deeper, or at least higher, than this one here. They need a lot more water than a flatboat. Well, the Hanna came in all right. But when she took some passengers and tried to go back down river, they run her aground right near here."

"So this is where the Robert Hanna sat, is it?" asked Mr. Whitaker.

"That's exactly where it sat," said Mr. McClure, "and for six months, too!"

Now all the men laughed. Bud stood up to get a better view of the river. There didn't seem to be anything sitting in it just now. He watched the rippling water of the shallows and hoped the flatboat wouldn't have such a bad time of it.

"All right, get on yer handles and get ready for it," said Mr. McClure. "Andrew, help Jacob with the rudder. See now? We'll want to get the boat just off to the center there, where the water's a bit darker-colored. That dark color means the water's deeper, son. The boat should get through there all right."

"All right."

Bud came closer in to the middle of the boat's roof. He sat down a few feet away from Andrew. Surely they would let Bud know if there was anything he could do.

"We're gettin' too close to shore."

"Take us back out a little, James."

"We're trying."

"Well, c'mon now!"

"Ethan, help us here!"

Bud got low to the planks beneath him. They were getting awfully close to the banks where the water was shallow.

Sna-A-A-A-G!

It was a long, loud, rough sound. The boat stopped. Water flowed on around them. Mr. McClure came from the other side of the boat. He looked out over the edge of the roof into the water. Bud went to the man's side and looked down, too. There, beneath them, they could see to the bottom of the river. The corner of the boat had lodged itself into the rocks and sand.

"Let's try the sweep."

Mr. McClure and Mr. Whitaker pushed against the bank with it. The boat did not budge. Ethan and Mr. Whitesman brought the other sweep over and tried to push on the bank, too. Nothing happened.

"Well, fellas . . . ," Mr. Bucher let himself down onto the gunnel facing the shore. He reached to the inside wall of the cabin. Out came the wooden plank they'd used for loading. "I think we're gonna have to unload!"

CHAPTER FIVE
Going to Town

The men laid the plank between the flatboat and the riverbank. They tied the boat to some nearby trees. Then came the *livestock*. Mr. McClure and Mr. Bucher began driving the calves and hogs across the plank and onto the bank. Once this was done, the crates were the next to leave the boat. The men toted them ashore and stacked them near the river's edge. All this while, Bud remained where he was on the roof of the flatboat.

"Let's try!" Mr. Bucher finally yelled.

They ran aboard and grabbed the sweeps.

"Heave, ho!" yelled Mr. Bucher.

Bud lowered himself against the boards. He'd be ready when the boat dislodged itself from the snag.

The men pushed with their sweeps and groaned. Nothing happened. They gripped the sweeps better and pushed once more:

"Heave, ho-o-o-o!"

Nothing.

Bud stood up and looked at Mr. McClure. He was frowning. He dropped the handle of his sweep. From out of the cabin below he brought another barrel. The other men did the same. Back and forth they went over the plank, taking more of their cargo ashore.

Bud wondered: should he get off the boat and watch the barrels and crates for them? There were sure to be plenty of mice and other varmints down here near the water. The least Bud could do was protect the cargo while it sat on the shore. He waited until no one was on the plank, and he hurried across it.

The sun shone down onto a grassy spot near the barrels. Bud sat down there. How nice it felt to be on still, sturdy land, again! He certainly preferred it to a boat. Bud knew what to expect from the ground. He knew how to find a comfortable spot. He knew how to cock back his ears and listen for little varmints by the unusual sounds they made. But everything on a boat was different! Bud stretched out his legs pleasantly and got comfortable in the dirt.

"Let's try again!" yelled Mr. Bucher.

They boarded the boat. Once again, the men stuck their sweeps against the bank.

"Heave, ho!"

Bud perked up his ears. The boat shifted!

"Heave, ho-o-o-o!"

The flatboat broke free from the snag. Once again, it rose and fell in the current. The ropes from the trees stretched tight. They were the only things holding the boat in place now.

Every one of the men smiled.

"Let's load up!" someone yelled.

Mr. McClure steadied the plank onto the boat again. The rest of the men dashed to the cluster of barrels and began loading them up.

Bud felt a pair of fingers scratch his head. He looked up. There was Andrew, grinning above him. In that instant, Bud forgot his dislike of boats. How could he resist all those smiles? Even Andrew was energetic, again. They were on their way to New Orleans!

The boy took a crate from the stack and carried it aboard. The other men came and went between the boat and the cargo on the shore. Bud stayed with the goods until the very last barrel was taken aboard. Then it was time for the livestock. Bud stepped back. He was in no hurry to get onto the boat with the hogs.

"Get on!"

"Oink! Oi-i-i-ink!"

"Get on!" Mr. Bucher yelled from one side of the hogs.

"Go on!" Mr. McClure yelled from the other side.

"Oi-i-i-ink!"

The hogs scurried around between the two men.

"Go on!"

"Oi-i-i-ink!"

Most of the hogs began making their way towards the plank. Two of them, however, broke away from the group and ran right towards Bud! He leapt out of their way. But when he'd landed and turned around, the hogs were coming at him, again!

"Meo-O-O-OW!"

"Bud?!"

Bud darted away from the bank. Still he could hear the hogs were just behind him. He knew they were scavengers. Hogs would eat anything! He'd never *heard* of hogs eating cats, but he wouldn't sit around and get trampled just to find out! Still running, Bud turned aside into the brush.

"Bud! Come back!"

"Let him go, son. He don't need to come with us down river."

The brush was thick, but still Bud ran.

"But, Pa, how will he get home?" Andrew was asking.

"He knows which way's which," returned the father. "He'll find his way home. We need to get this load down river now."

"But, Bud!"

Though Bud heard them, he paid no attention. The voices became quieter as he ran further and further from the river, into the grass and trees.

CHAPTER SIX
Bringing Home the Supper

The sun was getting low in the sky behind him when Bud finally slowed down. The sounds of the hogs and flatboat men had long since faded behind him. He supposed he could just wait a bit and then go back to the river. But no. He wouldn't return to the river. That was for sure! Close quarters with hogs and calves? That was no place for a cat! How would he have managed to take his afternoon naps? What would he have eaten on that long trip to New Orleans? What would he have done with himself? He was sorry to leave Andrew without so much as a goodbye. Bud was more than happy, though, to leave the boat to the men.

But then, if he didn't return to the river, what would he do? Where was he, after all? Bud sat down and sniffed the air. He could just barely catch a scent of the river behind him. Fields and pastures stretched out on either side of the road in front of him. Cows dotted the pastures. They held their heads low to the ground as they grazed. Up ahead of Bud sat a log cabin with its barn and outbuildings in the next lot. Nothing was familiar.

It was then that Bud knew he was lost. He'd never been lost before, and it was a terrible feeling! It was the time of day when he usually took a nap. But how could a cat nap like this, in a new place, not knowing where he was or what to expect? Besides, he was hungry! If only he were in Prairietown just then. He would've wandered over to the doctor's house, or else up to the Golden Eagle Inn, and waited for dinner scraps from the kitchen.

Dinner did feel like the most important thing just then. After that he could worry about getting home. And so, Bud lowered himself and stalked through the grass, looking and listening. When he came to a clearing at the edge of one of the fields, he stopped. It was a nice, large expanse of ground with some trees sprinkled about. It hadn't been plowed or planted, but simply left. Robins, just back for the spring, hopped here and there in the grass and pecked at the ground. Bud supposed they were in search of their own dinner. Bud, however, barely looked at them. For beyond them, roosting up in a tree, sat three wild turkeys!

They were all three hens, and they clucked back and forth to one another. The dark feathers on their backs glistened in the sun. Their wings were tucked nicely to their sides. Now these would make a fine dinner! Every now and then, patients had brought a turkey to Dr. Campbell's house to pay a medical bill. Bud would always stay close to the kitchen on days Abigail cooked one of them. She was sure to throw tasty bones and scraps out with her slop jar. Bud's stomach growled. If only he was home in Prairietown!

He set himself down in the grass a few feet from the tree.

"Squak, squak, squak," mumbled the hens. One of them stepped off of her branch. She flapped her wings and brought herself softly to the ground. Like the robins at the edge of the clearing, she started pecking here and there for food. Another hen came down from the tree to join her.

"Squak, squak, squak.."

The hens paid no attention to Bud as they ate. That was perfect. He got his back legs ready beneath and waited for the nearest hen to turn her back to him. Any minute he'd pounce on her from behind and . . .

"GO-O-O-OBLE, gobble, gobble!"

Bud looked up. A big Tom turkey came down on top of him. It must have been up in a nearby tree!

"GO-O-O-OBLE, gobble, gobble!"

Feathers flapped in Bud's face. He felt sharp pecks on his back.

"Meow!"

Bud backed away.

"GO-O-O-OBLE, gobble, gobble!"

The Tom's feathers blinded Bud. It kept just on top of him.

"GO-O-O-OBLE, gobble, gob—"

Bud spat and swatted his attacker with his paw. The Tom jumped back. Only then did Bud get a good look at it. It was a huge bird! The feathers at its tail stood out very full. The skin of its face and neck was bright blue with anger. Bud would never have tried to catch a hen if he had known this Tom was protecting her!

"GO-O-O-OBLE, gobble, gobble!"

It took three steps towards Bud. The red flap of skin over its beak flopped about with each step. Bud moved back. This was the first time he'd tried to catch a hen. It would certainly be the last. If only he could get away from this Tom!

"GO-O-O-OBLE, gobble, gobble!"

The Tom took a peck at Bud.

"GO-O-O-OBLE, gobble, gobble!"

Again it pecked. Bud jumped back. Its beak grabbed a tuft of Bud's yellow fur!

"Meow!"

"GO-O-O-OBLE, gobble, gobble!"

Bud ran. The turkey followed him, pecking each time Bud's tail was within reach.

"GO-O-O-OBLE, gobble, gob—"

Swat!

"Get on, you old Tom!"

Out of nowhere, a boy had come and swatted the Tom turkey with a long twig.

"GO-O-O-OBLE, gobble, gobble!"

The boy put himself between Bud and the Tom. He waved the twig and took several steps toward the turkey. The Tom stepped back.

"Get on now!"

"Gobble, gobble, gobble!"

"Go on before I tie you up and take you home for supper!"

"Gobble, gobble, gobble," said the Tom. It went back towards the hens, who'd gathered around the base of a small tree.

Bud rubbed against the boy's woolen trousers. His tail wouldn't have lasted the pecking much longer!

"You're welcome, little fella." The boy reached down to pet Bud. "I'd have tried for one o' those hens, myself, if I hadn't already got ma these fish for supper." He held up a line of fish fresh from the river. Now those would make a fine supper tonight!

He scratched Bud behind the ears one more time and stood up. Bud watched as the boy walked south. His line of fish dangled over his shoulder. Bud glanced back at the turkeys. They were up in a tree, again, roosting on its low branches. The Tom sat just beside the hens now. Bud looked back after the boy. There must have been nine or ten catfish on that line. If only he could manage to find the leavings from *that* supper! Well then, that was just what he would try.

Bud trotted after the boy. He followed him out onto the road and away from the setting sun.

CHAPTER SEVEN
Talk of the Town

The road was much larger than the Prairietown roads Bud was used to. It led them between fields, past log cabins and kitchen gardens. Every now and then the boy would look back over his shoulder. Each time, he saw Bud trotting along a safe but eager distance behind him. The boy finally stopped. Bud stopped, too.

"Come here, fella." The boy snapped his fingers.

Bud came closer and sniffed the outstretched hand. It smelled of fish and fields and barns, like Martin Zimmerman's hands at the end of a day.

"Are you tryin' to come home with me?"

There was something kind about the boy. Cats can sense such things. Bud rubbed against the boy's shin with his forehead.

"Well, I'm Josiah. Pleased to meet you, little fella. Come on with me, then. We'll probably have some scraps for you after supper tonight." Josiah beckoned Bud to follow. "We live up on Tennessee just off Washington Street here. You'll like it. We can even see the top of the State House to the West of us."

And so Bud followed Josiah along Washington Street. As they got closer into town, Bud realized he could not just walk casually in this street as he did along the Prairietown roads at home. The people walking along the street had to walk along the muddy edge. The center of the street seemed to belong to the horsemen who rode back and forth past them. After the first horse nearly trotted over the top of Bud, he was sure to stay close to Josiah's heels at the roadside.

Bud also began to see more buildings on either side of them. Frame buildings sided with wooden *clapboards* stood some yards back from the roadside. Some of them looked like homes with their kitchen gardens in nearby lots. Others seemed to belong to *tradesmen*. Bud sniffed the air. He was sure he smelled several different types of leather. There was a strong smell of a *tanner* working with skins. There was also a softer leather smell. Bud could have sworn a saddler was crafting his saddles in one of the buildings they passed.

Yet another frame building possessed a nice, large front window. It displayed broad-brimmed hats of many sizes and even a couple top hats. Top hats made of beaver fur, perhaps? They looked fine enough to be beaver. In fact, sniffing the building from the road, Bud could smell nothing but felt, beaver, and straw. Was this a *hatter's* place? Bud had never seen one before. A store selling only hats wouldn't get much business in a small place like Prairietown.

There were so many things to see and smell! Bud fell behind Josiah. When he realized the boy was no longer just in front of him, he panicked. He tried to sniff and find which way the boy had gone. But there were so many smells in the street he couldn't tell!

"Hey, little buddy!"

Bud turned around. Josiah had walked north up a different street. Bud hurried after him. This new street was narrower than Washington Street had been. Buildings, however, still rose from along the roadside. Some were even brick! One home at the far end of the block sat back a ways from a wrought iron fence. This was where Josiah stopped and waited for Bud to join him.

Bud stopped at his side and looked at this house. Two little *colonnades* framed its door. Windowpanes reflected the orange of the low sun from either side of these. Two pine trees stood in front of the building, rising above its roof. The place looked finer than even Dr. Campbell's house!

Josiah led Bud back along the fence to the side of the house. He opened a door near the back.

"Martha, look who's come to visit you!" he yelled.

They stepped into a warm kitchen. From between Josiah's legs, Bud could see a girl sitting on the far side of the hearth, facing them. She looked up from the sewing in her lap.

"Who is it, Joe?" she asked, peering around him to the outside.

Josiah, however, closed the door.

"Here!" He pointed down at Bud. "And here," he added, "is the supper I promised."

"Oh!" Martha ignored the fish. She ran over to pick up Bud. "May he stay?"

"If he likes. He's made himself my little buddy." Josiah scratched Bud's head. The boy then pulled off his green woolen over shirt and hung it on a nail behind the door. He began removing the fish from his line.

Martha took Bud back to the chair by the fire. She hugged him tightly. When she let him go, Bud curled up in her lap.

"You remind me of a mouser we had at home. I've missed him so much!"

"Didn't you see him when you visited your folks last month?" asked Josiah, lifting a steaming kettle from the hearth. He took it to the dry sink across the room, where he poured the hot water into a bowl. He must have been getting ready to scale the fish. Bud sure was ready for supper!

"Yes. But that was last month," she answered. "At home he kept us company every day when we sat down with our needlework at the fire. But since I've come to live in town . . . ," she let her voice trail off. She stopped petting Bud.

Josiah worked at the dry sink with his back to them. Bud, however, saw tears standing in Martha's eyes. They surprised him.

"Things are different workin' here in town, away from home," she continued, quietly. "But we need the help o' the extra money I earn here. I want to help, even if I miss home."

She lifted Bud up so she could look into his face.

"Where's your home, kitty? Huh?" she asked, touching her nose to

Bud's. "Where do you belong?"

The girl reminded him of Elizabeth Bucher. They looked about the same age. But Elizabeth always spoke with envy about her sister's chance to work in Prairietown. She'd have been excited for Martha's chance to live and work in Indianapolis! This was such a large kitchen with fancy, red and white china sitting in the press. Elizabeth would be jealous of all the fancies here, for sure!

Martha hugged Bud again. "I've missed kitty . . . ," she repeated.

Poor Martha. Weren't any of the things here important to her? He suddenly remembered the look on Abigail's face yesterday afternoon. Elizabeth had accused her sister of not understanding her wish for something different. But did she? Did Abigail feel like Martha sometimes, missing her family's home but doing her duty anyway?

Martha set Bud down. She wiped her eyes with the worn blue sleeve of her work dress. When she lowered her arm again, Bud licked the back of her hand. She'd get used to living in town. Bud was sure. Besides, with a helpful boy like Josiah around . . .

"Thanks, little friend," she whispered into his ear. She kissed the top of his head and stood up.

"You go on now," she said, going over to Josiah and pushing him aside from the dry sink.

"Thank you for cleaning these, but your brother's comin' back with the cows any time. He'll need your help puttin' 'em up. This is my work here."

Josiah laughed and dried his hands. "All right, then. See you at supper."

Bud watched Josiah leave through the back door. The boy's footsteps went down the wooden steps outside. Then they were gone. He lowered his head to the chair.

The next thing he knew, he smelled something wonderful. Was it . . . bread? He looked down at the hearth. The fire crackled and popped loudly. Flames surrounded four charred logs. Vivid orange-red coals glowed from a pile beneath them. Out a ways from the hearth, a *spider* sat on the bricks. Some of the orange-red coals glowed from on top of its lid and from underneath the pan, too. Bud remembered days in Prairietown. So often he'd sit in the chair by the Curtis family's fire. Mrs. Curtis would take the most delicious applesauce cakes out of her spider! Oh, he missed that! He knew how Martha felt, being away from her home.

"Ah, do you smell that?" Martha came to the fire. She took a hook hanging from the mantel and used it to lift the spider's lid. The smell of baking bread was instantly strong in his nose! Bud stood up and peered into the pan. A large, browning loaf nestled inside. He felt the emptiness of his stomach.

"Almost done," said Martha. She lowered the lid. "We'll just let the edges of the bread pull away from the sides of the pan. Then we know its done all the way through."

Bud sat down again on the chair and tried to close his eyes. It was no use, though. He couldn't hope to sleep with supper so close!

"Martha?" asked a voice from behind them. They turned around. The door from the front of the house was open. A woman with a black shawl stood in the doorway.

Bud drew himself behind the back of the chair to hide.

"Did Josiah bring us enough fish?" the woman asked.

"Yes, Mrs. Brown," answered Martha. "I expect he did."

"Remember, we've some lemon balm drying from the ceiling over there. Mr. Brown does like it with his fish."

"Yes, ma'am. I've already sprinkled some in the pan."

"That's a good girl, Martha." Mrs. Brown smiled and laid her hand on the girl's shoulder. "You're such a help. I'm surprised your family parted with you. But you'll more than earn your 80 cents a week here. I know you're being a great help to your family, too."

Bud leaned around the back of the chair to look at Martha. The girl smiled broadly at Mrs. Brown's praise. Bud was glad to see her happy.

"What's that?" Mrs. Brown asked suddenly. She pointed to Bud. He pulled himself back behind the chair again.

"A mouser, ma'am."

He heard uncertainty in Martha's voice. Bud hoped he wouldn't get her in trouble.

"Mr. Josiah brought it home this evening," continued Martha.

"Dear, just today I've been frightened out of my wits with a mouse in the parlor! The parlor, of all places!"

The woman came around to look at Bud. She scratched his head. He began to purr. She picked him up and wiped his feet with a rag. It tickled as she wiped between his toes. Bud tried to pull his feet away from her. The woman continued, though, saying:

"Let's bring him into the parlor and see what he won't do for us."

Martha smiled at Bud as he was carried past her.

Mrs. Brown took him through a dining room and then into a cozy parlor. A fire burnt in the hearth at the far end of the room. A sofa, chairs, and some tables sat up against the walls. Mrs. Brown set Bud down in a corner near the hearth. He looked around.

There was a crack in the corner. It grew wide at the bottom of the wall near the floor. It certainly was big enough for a mouse to fit through. Oh yes! Bud could smell the scent of a mouse. This must be its home.

Mrs. Brown went to a rocking chair at the other side of the hearth. She took up a pair of spectacles and some linen pieces from the *sewing table.* For a moment, Bud couldn't bring himself to look back at the hole. Was this parlor as fancy as Dr. Campbell's parlor? Bud had never been in the Campbell parlor. Mrs. Campbell wouldn't allow it. She said she'd have no "livestock" in her husband's house. Bud looked about him at the colorful room with its soft, comfortable things. He suspected only the mouse's presence had allowed him into this parlor. Oh well. He'd earned his place on the flatboat with a mouse, too. Martha had her work in the kitchen. Bud had his work here.

He looked back at the hole. Nothing stirred at the moment. He'd leap into the soft seat of a chair closer to the hearth. He'd be out of sight from the mouse's hole and could listen for it well enough. Bud hopped up and laid himself down. He cocked his ears towards the hole in the corner.

The fire rasped and even whistled. Mrs. Brown breathed a deep, regular breath as she rocked back and forth in her creaky rocking chair. Bud lifted his head. He heard something else. What was it? It came from outside. Horses, Bud thought. Mrs. Brown looked up at the window. She must have heard it, too, for she stood up and hurried out by the dining room door. When she returned, she was carrying a tray. She brought the smell of coffee with her. When she set the tray down, Bud saw the tall, red and white coffeepot. Mrs. Brown began pouring steaming brown liquid into the matching cups.

"Right this way, John," said a voice from outside.

Bud looked quickly at the hall door. It wasn't the door Mrs. Brown had used. He'd hardly noticed it. But now it opened, and two men entered.

"Thanks, Alex," said the man in front to the one behind him.

"What is this, dear? Coffee?" asked the second man.

"Yes, Mr. Brown," answered his wife. "I thought something special for tonight. There's nothing like it to warm the insides."

"Quite right! And we've certainly got reason to celebrate tonight!" answered her husband.

"Mr. Elder, welcome," said the woman to her guest. She handed him a steaming cup and saucer. "Cream or sugar?"

"Thank you, ma'am. Cream."

Mr. Elder took a seat against the wall where Bud's chair sat. Mr. Brown, with his cup in hand, went to Bud's chair.

"What's this?" he asked, looking at Bud.

"I brought him in to see after a mouse, dear."

"Is he ours?"

"Josiah brought him home today."

Mr. Brown nodded. "He's welcome to see after the mouse from anywhere but my chair."

The man picked Bud up by the scruff of his neck and dropped him to the floor. The floorboards were chilly on the pads of Bud's paws! Immediately, he jumped up into the next chair he could reach. It had a harder, wooden seat and felt almost cold to the touch. It wasn't so near to the fire as the other chair was. Bud had to wrap his tail around his feet to get warmer.

"How's business at the Inn, Mr. Elder?" asked Mrs. Brown, returning to her rocker.

"Well, ma'am, thank you," answered the guest. He paused to sip his coffee. "But then, I've just been telling Alex that I plan to leave the business shortly. I've notified the owner to look out for a new proprietor."

"No?" Mrs. Brown looked up from her sewing, disappointment on her face.

"Yes, ma'am. The area's growing. With all the *Internal Improvements Bill* calls for, there'll be plenty of building to be done."

"Building's his trade, dear," reminded Mr. Brown.

"Indeed, do tell what the board has decided tonight!" asked Mrs. Brown, forgetting the knitting in her lap as she turned to her husband. "I've been positively feverish since January's bill to know what money they'd put aside for it."

"Two million," answered Mr. Brown.

"Two million?!"

"Yes, Mrs. Brown," jumped in Mr. Elder. "The Board of Internal Improvements has tonight made the provision of two million dollars for improving our roads and building canals to connect us with the east. Just imagine the trade and travel this will bring!"

"And building," added Mr. Brown with a wink.

"Mrs. Brown," continued the guest with wide eyes, "Indiana will be exalted among the states of this country!" He sent his hand into the air with excitement. The saucer he held with it sloshed his coffee over the side of its cup. A few of the hot drops landed on Bud's tail.

"Meow!"

Bud screamed and leapt to a farther chair.

"Mr. Elder, please!" scolded the hostess, concerned for the parlor furniture.

"Please forgive me, Mrs. Brown." Mr. Elder dabbed at the arm of the chair with his handkerchief.

The dining room door creaked. It was Martha. Bud forgot his stinging tail. He knew what her presence meant!

"If you'll excuse me, ma'am, dinner is served," offered the girl quietly.

"Thank you, Martha."

"Shall we?" asked Mr. Brown.

"Oh yes!" answered Mr. Elder, perhaps a little too quickly. He seemed glad to have attention drawn away from his dripping coffee cup.

The three rose from their chairs and left the parlor. Martha hurried over to Bud's chair.

"I've got some nice bones for you in the kitchen, little buddy."

Martha patted his head, but Bud didn't stop to purr. He hopped off the hard wooden chair and hurried to the kitchen.

CHAPTER EIGHT
Working Days

A rustling sound near his ears woke Bud the next morning. He opened one eye. The sun was already rising. He stretched out a paw across the wooden step and opened the other eye. Josiah Brown sat on the ground beside the steps.

"You missed breakfast, Buddy!" said the boy. He had papers in his lap that he was rolling into a tube. "Martha left out some scraps for you." He nodded his head towards the back gate.

Bud, however, didn't turn his head to look for the scraps. He was watching Josiah. The boy must have had some sort of newspaper or magazine. Bud caught sight of some bold letters at the top. "Black . . . ," it began. Was it a *Blackwood's Magazine*? Yes, Bud saw the rest of the title now. He'd seen those before. But why was the boy tying a scrap of ribbon around it? And why was he trying to tie the ribbon into a bow?

Josiah still struggled with the ribbon when the latch of the kitchen door lifted. He shoved the magazine behind him and started pulling at his shoestrings. Martha emerged from the door. She had an old shawl around her shoulders and a basket in her arms.

"Joe! I didn't know you were back from the pastures."

"Just got back," he said, his attention still on his shoe strings. "Had no trouble takin' the cows out except for these shoes. The strings won't stay tied!"

Martha smiled and watched him adjust the strings. Bud strolled down the path to the gate. He sniffed the pile of scraps. Skins off of side meat! He sat down and chewed at the pieces while he watched the boy and the girl. Joe still tugged at his shoestrings. Martha still waited for him to look up and talk with her more. He did neither.

"Well," said Martha finally. "Your ma sent me on some errands. I'm headed over to Yandes' store."

"See you tonight, then." Joe still didn't look up.

"'Bye, Joe."

Martha seemed a little disappointed. She walked to the gate and paused to unlatch it. Bud heard a scratching noise above him. He looked up. It didn't seem to be a noise Martha had made. It wasn't the noise of shoes scraping along a dirt path, either. It was more like . . .

A mouse! Bud saw a little, whiskered nose stuck out through a gap in the bottom of Martha's basket.

"Meow!" Bud stood up and pawed at the hem of her skirt. She looked down.

"Are you comin', too? Silly kitty. Come on before I close the gate."

She didn't understand. Bud followed her out through the gate. She stopped to latch it back.

"Meow!" He pawed at her skirt and tried to reach up at the basket.

The mouse pulled its nose back up through the gap. Bud pawed at the basket's bottom.

"Yes, Buddy, you can come!" Martha scratched his head and then walked north up Tennessee Street.

Bud followed. How would he make her understand? Martha must have something tasty in the basket, or else the mouse wouldn't have gotten in there. He had to get that mouse out before it ate her goodies! If only Bud could get her to let the basket down.

They were up to the next street in no time. Martha turned right.

"Meow!" Bud swatted at her basket.

"Stay down, kitty. I know these cakes smell good . . . ," she patted the basket, "but Mrs. Brown sent these for Mrs. Yandes. We can't have any." Martha walked on.

Bud followed her, all the time walking just underneath the basket. Every now and then the mouse would poke its nose between the slats and draw it back up again quickly. Finally, Martha glanced down at Bud.

"Kitty," she said, picking him up. "You can't have the cakes. Now look here . . . ," she pointed ahead of them. "Look at all you're missin' starin' at the basket all this time. See? We're comin' to the circle."

Indeed, ahead of them the straight road opened out onto a curve that circled a large space of land. Brick and frame buildings lined the outside of the circle. Men in top hats strode along the edges of this circle street. A wagon or two even passed along the center! To the inside of all this stood a large, square building of yellowish-colored brick. It had a grand, imposing entryway. Bud's eyes rose up along the structure. It was a full two stories high! And there, on top of the very roof, was a flat area surrounded by a low *balustrade*. Now if only Bud could have climbed his way up there. He could just imagine the sunny afternoon naps to be had there!

"The governor's mansion . . . ," whispered Martha, following Bud's eyes.

The two of them had paused. A man on horseback rode past them in the street, and Martha nudged Bud off to the side. She squatted down beside Bud, still gazing at the mansion:

"Isn't it beautiful?" She set her basket down. "Of course, no governor's ever lived there. I heard the last governor's wife refused to. She didn't want her drying laundry to be on display in the middle of town! I think . . ."

Bud's attention was no longer on Martha or the mansion. He was staring at her basket. The mouse peeked its little nose out over the rim. The whiskers twitched as it sniffed the air. There was its head! It lifted one foreleg out over the basket's edge. As soon as the next leg emerged, Bud swatted the little stowaway to the ground.

"Oh!" cried Martha, jumping up to her feet.

The mouse darted out into the road. Bud ran after it, going north and then east along the circle.

"Kitty, be careful!" yelled Martha.

The varmint zig-zagged back and forth along the road, but Bud stayed

just behind it. There was a woman in the yard of one of the houses near by. She'd just flung a blue-striped tick over the fence and begun beating the dust and dirt out of it with a paddle. Bud was almost on top of the mouse when it darted over to the tick and crawled up its blue and white side.

"Oh!" cried the woman. She tried to swat the mouse off the tick. She just missed it. When she tried again, she just missed Bud as he leapt onto the tick, himself!

"OH!" she cried again.

The mouse balanced its way several feet along the fence before it jumped off into the road. Bud did the same. Down the road it ran, causing a horse to whinny and rear with its rider. Bud met the mouse on the other side of the horse. He brought his paws down quickly, almost on top of it. He missed! They ran past the church and were at the north side of the circle before Bud knew it.

He had to catch that mouse soon or he'd lose it! It was headed straight towards a one-story, frame building just inside the circle. The mouse must have known of a chink or hole somewhere in the brick foundation, for it seemed to move faster and faster the closer it got. It knew right where it was going! The mouse scurried under the rail fence. Bud leapt to the top of the fence to go over after it.

"Moo-o-o-o!"

Bud caught his balance at the top of the rail. He was face to face with a cow on the other side!

"Moo-o-o-o!"

Bud felt the cow's breath on his face, and he froze.

"Buddy!"

Bud was snatched back off the fence rail. It was Martha! She held him tightly under her arm. She carried him quickly along the edge of the road. Men and women stared as they passed. Bud, however, felt the muscles in his body relax.

"Don't you cause such a ruckus down town," she mumbled harshly as they reached the south side of the circle. They took the straight road leading away from it. "Disturbin' the fine lady's beddin', nearly throwin' a horseman, and then headin' towards the house with the new fire engine! What do you think they'd have done with you if they'd caught you?!"

Bud hid his nose in the crook of Martha's arm. He was sorry he'd caused such a commotion. He just wanted to stop that mouse from sneaking and thieving any more!

"I'm sorry, little fella," she said after a while.

Bud lifted his head. Martha scratched him behind the ears.

"I'm awfully glad you got that mouse out of Mrs. Yandes' cakes. Mrs. Brown would surely be, too. It's just that you scared me somethin' awful. There's lots of important things goin' on at the circle. Menfolk are doin' business in their shops up there. The government offices are in that mansion. I was afraid someone or somethin' important was goin' to get hurt—particularly you!"

Bud licked her hand. She was a good girl. Soon they came across a wider street. It was as wide as the one that he and Josiah had taken the day before—Washington Street, the boy had said. Martha turned onto it, carrying Bud with her. They'd only gone a little ways when she stopped and held Bud up to the glass front window of a frame building.

"See, kitty. Look!"

Bud saw counters, barrels, and shelves of all kinds. Cloth, ribbons, pots, dishes, hats, tools, brooms and brushes—Bud could hardly take everything in! But Martha pointed somewhere specific. Bud followed her finger. There, on a shelf near the window, was a row of books. A stack of newspapers and magazines sat beside them. One of the smaller magazines leaned up against the back of the shelf so they could see its front. Bud was sure he'd seen it somewhere before. Yes, it was *Blackwood's Magazine*!

"Look at all those books and newspapers. Oh, Kitty, I wish I could read better than I do. I only learnt a little from my brothers. But in the evenings they'd read aloud to the family. They always seemed to find old copies of *Blackwood's*. I loved the stories, especially. There were romances. There were adventures to cities and castles. Those stories could take us anywhere!"

Martha fell silent and gazed through the window at the shelf.

"Josiah caught me here one day looking through one of the *Blackwood's*. I knew I wouldn't be able to read much of it, but I just wanted to see the pictures and feel the pages. I was supposed to be runnin' errands for Mrs. Brown. I was afraid he'd tell her how I was dawdlin' and not doin' my work. He hasn't said anything about it since. I think he's givin' me another chance."

Was that why Josiah didn't want her to see the magazine he was tying up? Bud looked up at Martha's face. She stared longingly at the *Blackwood's Magazine* on display. Suddenly, Bud understood what Josiah had been doing with that magazine. The boy was going to give it to Martha! Why else would he have been tying ribbon around it and making a pretty bow?

Bud licked Martha's hand. She'd see why Josiah hadn't said anything. He was going to surprise her with a copy of her own!

Martha shook herself from her thoughts. "I shouldn't dawdle now!" She set Bud down on the ground. "I'll be right back!"

She disappeared into the store. Bud set himself in the dirt under the window. He laid his chin on his paws and closed his eyes. Footsteps walked here and there in front of him. Horses' hooves pawed at the mud in the street. He heard one set of hooves come awful close, and he opened his eyes. A man was tying his horse to a post nearby.

Bud stood up nervously. He'd always liked to nap in front of Mr. Whitaker's store in Prairietown. It was a pleasant place. But Indianapolis was different. The road in front of the store didn't quite feel as safe. Bud looked around. When the store's door opened again, he slipped inside.

The chilly March air was replaced with the stale, inside air heated by a coal stove. Bud sniffed the area around him. Someone must have brought raccoon skins to trade with. He could smell leather and fur somewhere. He almost went to explore these smells, but he stopped. He'd get a closer look at the *Blackwood's Magazine* first. Martha had been so intent upon it.

He leapt up to the window ledge and then up further to the top of the counter. There it was, a magazine whose front looked very much like the one Josiah had. This must have been the latest copy of the magazine. Its pages looked fresh and crisp . . .

"Cat, what're ya doin' there? Get down."

Bud felt himself lifted up from behind and turned around in the air. His muscles were tense. He was ready to struggle free of the grasp until he saw who held him. It was Martin Zimmerman!

CHAPTER NINE
Old Friends

Martin Zimmerman's eyes widened. Bud meowed and licked Martin's hand.

"Bud?!"

Martin set Bud on the floor and squatted down next to him. Bud rubbed his head against the boy's knee. It was so good to see him! But what was he doing all the way down here in Indianapolis?

"Why, little fella, what are *you* doin' here? I could've sworn I saw you . . . well . . . I saw you two days ago. You came down with Mr. Curtis when he hired us for this trip. But how'd you get down here?"

Bud just purred, glad to see Martin. Martin stared at Bud, seeming too surprised at first to say anything else. The boy finally spoke, saying:

"I'm glad I decided to stop by Yandes' store or we'd never have crossed paths! Richard and Jonathan are down at Jackson Brothers' for Mr. Curtis' *iron stock*. I slipped away to find something for Elizabeth Bucher. I wanted to . . . ,"

Martin paused and blushed. "She's always talkin' about town life and fancy things. She was lookin' so sad yesterday, I thought I'd bring her back somethin' special."

The door opened behind them.

"Martin!" Richard Zimmerman stuck his head inside the store. "Martin, we're leavin' now. Hurry up!"

The storekeeper and one of his customers stared at the door and then at Martin. Martin had a worried look on his face. He stood up. There, just before him, was the new copy of *Blackwood's Magazine* facing out from the shelf. Bud saw Martin smile. The boy grabbed the copy of the magazine and hurried up to the storekeeper at the far counter. He paid for the magazine and rushed back to the door.

"Come on, Bud. You wanna come back with us to Prairietown, don't you?" Martin was already outside, holding the door open.

Bud froze. Where was Martha? He couldn't see her anywhere. Had she gone to find Mrs. Yandes? Bud stood and rubbed against the doorframe, thinking. Martha didn't really need him to stay. He'd chased away Mrs. Brown's mouse. He wouldn't be able to keep Martha company anymore. But then, it looked like Josiah had some reading in mind for her these days. The boy would be good company for her. She'd get used to her new place soon. Besides, Bud was awfully ready to go home. Flatboat roofs, fancy parlors, busy Indianapolis streets—these were just not the places for him. He missed Prairietown!

That decided it. Bud hurried out the door Martin held open for him.

"What were you doin' in there, boy?" asked Richard Zimmerman.

He sat on one of the horses in front of the Zimmerman wagon. Their brother, Jonathan, stood in the street.

"Come on. The sky's lookin' dark now. We need to get as far as we can before any rain comes."

Martin jumped up and hung from the side of the wagon. He had his poke in one hand. It had an unusual rectangular shape. He must have slipped the copy of *Blackwood's* in there. He laid it carefully in one corner of the wagon bed. Martin let himself down and picked up Bud.

"Do you want to ride in here or walk with us, little fella?"

"Martin, don't bring that cat into the wagon."

"But Richard, it's Bud!"

"Bud?" Richard turned around in his saddle to look back at them.

"Bud!" Jonathan took him from Martin's hands. "What are you doin' here, little fella?" He held Bud up for Richard to see.

"Well I'll be switched!" said Richard, lifting his black felt hat and brushing his hair back underneath it. "Those are Bud's eyes, all right. I'd know 'em anywhere. But what in tarnation is he doin' here?"

Bud purred as Jonathan scratched his chin. That was a question that wouldn't be answered until the flatboat men returned from New Orleans next month!

"Well, come along, Bud. We'd better get you home. Ma'd hate to lose a good mouser like you from the Golden Eagle barn." He turned back around in his saddle and took up the horses' reigns in his hand. "Let's go!"

Jonathan set Bud down in the wagon *bed.*

"Ha!" yelled Richard.

The wagon lurched forward. They were on their way!

Bud glanced out over the back of the wagon. Martin and Jonathan walked along behind, talking and laughing. Bud lowered himself into the wagon again. Beneath him were pieces and pieces of iron stock. They were the long, thin, black bars that Mr. Curtis always used in his blacksmith's shop. Behind Bud, in the back of the wagon, were a couple coarse linen sacks stitched closed at the top. Balancing himself on the iron stock, Bud went back and sniffed the sacks. Rice!

"What'd you find, Bud?" Jonathan hung by his arms from the back of the wagon, looking in. "Oh, they're just some extra *dry goods* for Mr. Whitaker. He thought he didn't buy enough last time he was in Cincinnati."

Jonathan patted Bud and dropped himself back down onto the street.

Bud curled up against the sacks and enjoyed the lulling rhythm of the wagon wheels. He closed his eyes. The sun warmed his fur. The wind he heard above him didn't reach him down inside the wagon. Before long, he felt himself drifting off . . .

CLUNK-clunk!

The wagon jostled. Bud gripped the iron beneath him with his claws. What was that?

Bud crawled up to the edge of the wagon and looked over. Jonathan and Martin walked behind. Every now and then one of them picked up a stone to throw at a distant tree, or else a stick to drag along beside them.

CLUNK-clunk!

The wagon jolted, again. Bud steadied himself against the iron.

CLUNK-clunk!

The wagon moved on. Bud climbed back up to look over the edge of the wagon. There behind them, moving further into the distance with each second, was a cluster of tree stumps. Some of those stumps were a foot high!

CLUNK-clunk!

The wagon jolted again. Another stump emerged from beneath the wagon. Jonathan stepped over it with playfulness. Martin picked up his speed and came closer to the back of the wagon.

"Want to walk with us, Bud?" he asked.

"We won't have a very smooth ride now we're out of Indianapolis," Richard called back from the front of the wagon. "Fort Wayne-Indianapolis Pike's well traveled. We sink down in all the ruts and have a hard time missin' the stumps. State ain't had the money or workers to clear the stumps out yet."

So that was why Mr. Brown and Mr. Elder were so excited last night! The state was going to be able to tear out the stumps and smooth down the roads. Bud would have been as excited as Mr. Elder was if he'd known what it was like to travel on the Fort Wayne-Indianapolis Pike!

"Come on, Bud." Martin held his hands out to Bud from behind the wagon.

Bud lifted himself up to his full height against the edge of the wagon. He was nervously watching the ground move beneath him when Martin grabbed him.

"There!" Martin set Bud down on the ground.

Bud sniffed the dirt in the road. Wagon wheels, horse hooves, feet—he could smell all sorts of people who'd passed this way! The ground was nearly dry. But then, it wasn't dry enough to be dusty. There was still too much moisture from the thawing frost of winter.

Bud looked up. The Zimmermans were far ahead of him. He ran to catch

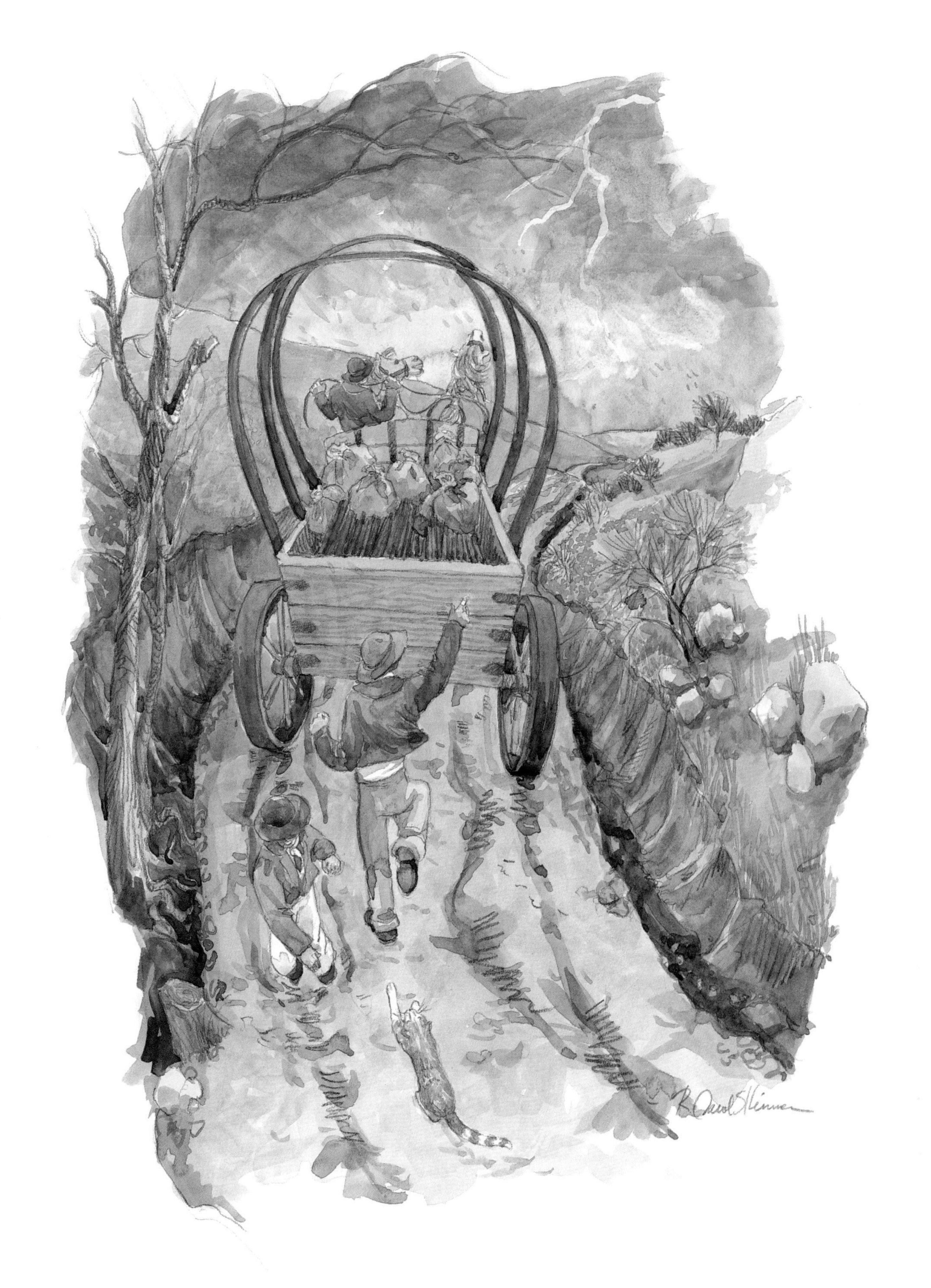

up, leaping over the stumps in his path. He was sure to stay in the middle of the road to avoid the ruts and ridges that were worn into it. When he caught up with Martin and Jonathan, he slowed to a trot.

Clank-CLANK!

Ahead of them, the wagon lurched over another stump. It rolled on.

The three of them followed behind as the afternoon sun got lower in the sky. It was about the time when Bud was craving something for supper that he noticed the wind. It had picked up. It gusted down in their faces from the north. Bud, in fact, thought he could smell rain in the air.

"Yup," said Martin after a minute. He pointed ahead of them. "The sky's getting' dark up there."

The wagon rode on, and they followed. Even when large, cold drops began falling from the sky, they continued at the same pace. The drops became heavier. Up ahead of them, they saw the sky light up for an instant before it returned to darkness. Lightning. Then the sky rumbled. They walked on.

Finally, rain began to pour. Bud ran ahead until he was walking under the wagon. Though his paws still got wet in the muddy road, at least his fur kept dry. In another moment, a bolt of lightning streaked across the sky. A sharp, loud clap of thunder roared all around them. Bud jumped. The horses at the front of the wagon paused. They whinnied and stepped back and to the side and back again. Bud darted out from under the wagon, scared the wheels would roll over his tail!

Lightning streaked, again, and the thunder clapped. The horses reared up on their back legs. Richard jumped off his horse and began unhitching them from the wagon. He led them off to the side of the road. He found a thick, low tree—low enough that lightning would never strike it—and stood with the horses underneath it. Martin and Jonathan crawled underneath the wagon. Bud joined them. They'd just settled themselves to watch the rain falling around them when Martin gasped and crawled out from underneath. Bud and Jonathan watched as he climbed up into the wagon.

"What're you doin'?"

They could hear Martin scrounging around above them in the bed of the wagon. Finally he climbed out and joined them underneath. He held something inside his over shirt. Bud could see, peeking out from underneath the shirt, the dirty brown cloth of Martin's poke. He must have been afraid Elizabeth's magazine would get wet!

"What's wrong?" Richard yelled from where he stood with the horses.

Nie-e-e-egh! called the horses, still worried by the thunder.

"What you got there, Martin?" asked Jonathan.

"Just my poke."

"What's so important in your poke?"

"Nothin'."

"You were in the store buyin' somethin' for Elizabeth Bucher, weren't you?"

"I was not!"

"You get her ribbons or somethin' nice?"

"I didn't get anything!"

"What's wrong?" yelled Richard from between thunder claps.

"Martin's just worried about the fancies he bought for the Bucher girl!" yelled Jonathan.

Even with the roaring thunder, they could all hear Richard Zimmerman laugh.

"I am not!" Martin crawled off to one corner of the wagon. He frowned and clutched the poke to his chest. Bud went over to rub against Martin's leg. He felt sorry for the boy. It was a shame people teased each other. Bud saw the men teasing each other all winter in the tap room of the Golden Eagle Inn, or else as they stood around the wood stove in Mr. Whitaker's store. He supposed people would be teasing Elizabeth, too, when they saw her with the magazine. Bud licked Martin's hand. He knew that when Martin gave Elizabeth that *Blackwood's Magazine*, neither of them would care a lick about all the teasing in the world. It would be all right. Martin would see.

"Thanks, Bud," whispered the boy.

He petted Bud for a long while as the thunder grew quieter and the lightning stopped. The horses, too, grew quiet. Eventually, they saw the sun throwing out a few rays from behind the clouds. Only a light drizzle still fell. They heard Richard bringing the horses towards them. The two brothers crawled out from underneath the wagon. Bud followed. He didn't care how much they slipped and slid on the muddy road north. They were going home!

CHAPTER TEN
Adventuring Home

It was dark when they reached Prairietown that evening. Bud had never been so glad to see the Golden Eagle Inn in all his life! They pulled around the side of the big, white building. The boys' mother, Mrs. Zimmerman, walked out onto the back porch. She was drying her hands on a towel.

"I was worried about you when the storm came through!" she called out to them from the porch steps.

"We were all right, Ma," responded Jonathan. "We just had to watch Martin. He got up into the wagon in the middle of the storm 'cause he was afraid his ribbons . . . hey!"

Martin elbowed his brother in the side.

"Martin!" scolded Mrs. Zimmerman. "Be nice to your brother! Now go help Richard with the horses."

The two boys went off to help their brother in the barn. Mrs. Zimmerman had half-turned to go back into the kitchen when she stopped. She saw Bud.

"Bud! Where've you been?" She came down off the porch and picked him up. She scratched his chin. "I was waitin' for you all yesterday! We got a varmint in the dinin' room again." She headed back inside the Inn with Bud still in her arms. "We'll get you some supper scraps right there in the dinin' room so you can watch for that mouse."

The mouse didn't emerge that night, but Bud slept long and deep when it was time for bed. The sun was already high in the sky when he awoke the next morning, ready to watch again for the mouse. He laid where he was for a moment, listening to the familiar sounds from inside the Inn. He was glad to be home. No wonder he'd slept so comfortably!

"Psst. Elizabeth, come here!"

Bud cocked his ear back. Was that Martin's voice? He looked out into the yard. Elizabeth Bucher was strolling up River Road with a basket on her arm.

"Elizabeth, come here!"

She stopped and looked over at the barn.

"Martin?"

"Come here a minute!" Bud saw Martin peeking out the barn doors.

"The Campbells sent me down with some things for your ma. They want to see the guests fed well at their Inn!" She smiled, but then she became serious. "Abigail told me to hurry back when I was done. I can't stop too long."

No less, Elizabeth wandered over to the barn and stopped in the doorway. She leant back against the open door. Bud thought he could still see a bit of a frown left on her face from the other day.

Bud wandered over, too, and sat at Elizabeth's feet. They both watched Martin. He was in the far corner of the barn. His hand scrounged around under a *bale* of hay, which was drying from the autumn before. Out came Martin's poke. Bud knew what the boy was doing!

"Did you have a good time in Indianapolis?" asked Elizabeth, looking impatient.

"Goin' down was fine. The trip back wasn't very good, though. It was a lot of work." Martin opened his poke as he talked.

"That doesn't matter. You still got to see the town. Indianapolis must have so many nice things!"

"Well, haulin' things for people pays good, so I'm glad to help with it. As for Indianapolis, it's got more people and more *mechanics*. It's got more stores and big buildings. But that's all. There're things it doesn't have, too."

"Like what?"

"Well, I don't know many people down there. Richard and Jonathan were loadin' all the time. It isn't so special seein' things down there without your friends to enjoy the place. I'd rather have an afternoon here."

Elizabeth didn't look convinced. "I don't see what good an afternoon here is when you could be in Indianapolis."

"Well," said Martin, holding *Blackwood's Magazine* out to her, "you could read . . ."

"*Blackwood's*! Oh, Martin!"

She snatched it from his hands and sat herself down on a stool near the door. Martin sat down on the ground beside her. They both read quietly. Bud could imagine Martha and Josiah sitting together just like this down in Indianapolis.

Elizabeth pointed to something on a page. Martin smiled. What was it? Bud went over and hopped up onto Elizabeth's lap. There were only a bunch of words on the pages. He looked up at his friends. They didn't even look at him. They certainly didn't offer to pet him! Bud put his paw on the page to get their attention.

"No, Bud." Elizabeth pulled him back against her. She kissed the top of his head but kept on reading.

Bud curled up on her lap. She began to pet him with the hand that was not holding the magazine. Martin started petting him with one hand, too. The boy saved the other hand to turn the magazine pages when they were ready. Bud closed his eyes and snuggled his nose into Elizabeth's dress. He'd rather be here than traveling on any flatboat, wagon, or Indianapolis street. Somehow, he thought Elizabeth just might agree with him at this moment. Whatever adventures she found in those pages, Elizabeth looked as happy as she could be, sitting there with her friend.

"Martin!" yelled Mrs. Zimmerman from outside.

Martin and Elizabeth jumped up. Bud fell to the ground.

"Martin, have you seen any of the Buchers? Mrs. Campbell was supposed to send some butter over this morning."

"I've got to go!" said Elizabeth, taking up her basket in one hand and clutching the magazine in the other. "I'll try to get away later. We can finish the story then." She tried to give the magazine back to Martin, but Martin shook his head.

"It's for you."

"For me?"

"Yes."

Elizabeth's eyes got big, and then her smile grew just as wide. She kissed the boy on the cheek and ran out of the barn, calling back: "Thank you!"

Bud looked up at Martin. The boy was smiling, and his cheeks were suddenly very red. He reached down to scratch Bud behind the ears. Then he stood up, saying:

"Let's get to work, little fella!"

GLOSSARY

bale— A bale is a large bundle of something pressed and tied up.

balustrade— A balustrade is a row of posts that hold up a railing.

bed— The bed of a wagon is the flat bottom inside where things are carried.

clapboards— Clapboards were flat wooden boards used for things like the siding on a building.

colonnades— Colonnades are rows of columns.

country sugar— Country sugar is another name for maple sugar.

dry goods— Dry goods are foods like rice, flour, and salt that do not go bad very quickly.

dry sink— A dry sink was a stand where women washed dishes. Houses in 1836 did not have faucets or running water inside. People had to heat a kettle of water by the fire and then pour the warm water into bowls on top of the dry sink for dishwater.

gee— "Gee" means left. When working with animals in the fields, farmers would often use this term when they wanted an animal to turn to the left.

grist mill— A grist mill was a place where people could take things like corn or wheat to be ground into corn meal or flour. Mills were located on river banks to make use of the water to power the machines.

gunnel— The gunnels are the upper edges of a flatboat's two longer sides. They are two of the largest, heaviest pieces of wood making up a flatboat.

haw— "Haw" means right. Farmers would use this term with work animals when they wanted them to turn to the right.

hogsheads— A hogshead is a large barrel.

Internal Improvements Bill— Indiana passed an Internal Improvements Bill in January of 1836. It called for the repair of Indiana's roads and the further construction of roads, railroads, and canals within the state. The Board of Internal Improvements, however, didn't decide on the funding for the bill until March of 1836.

iron stock— Iron stock are long bars of iron that blacksmiths bought to use in their shops. This was the iron they worked with to make everything they sold.

kettle holder— We would call these "pot holders" today.

lemon balm— Lemon balm is a type of mint many people grew in their gardens and used for cooking. It's leaf actually smells like lemon!

livestock—Livestock are animals raised to be sold or kept for use on a farm.

mechanics— (see tradesmen)

poke— Any sort of cloth bag was called a "poke."

reins— Reins are narrow straps of leather attached to the bit (bar) in a horse's mouth. Horses wore reins and bits when people rode them. Riders held the other ends of the reins in their hands. They used the reins to control the horses.

rudder— The rudder helped men steer the flatboat. A long wooden log went down into the water. At the bottom of the log was a broad, flat piece of wood. When the men moved the log from the roof, the flat piece moved in the water to guide the boat.

sewing table— A sewing table was a small piece of furniture. It had drawers underneath the table top where ladies could keep needles, thread, scissors, and other sewing supplies.

shallows— A section of a river in which the water is unusually shallow.

sledge— A sledge is a type of sled or sleigh that could carry a load of things over dirt, ice, snow, and other surfaces.

slop jar— Garbage and table scraps were put in a slop jar. When the jar was full, people would throw its contents out for hogs or other animals to eat.

spider— A spider is an iron pan with long legs which allow coals to be placed underneath it. When Martha baked bread, she put a lid on top of her spider and placed coals on top of the lid, also. That way, the pan was hot on the top and the bottom and the bread inside would bake evenly.

sweeps— Sweeps were long oars the boatmen used to steer the flatboat.

tanner— A tanner was a man whose work was to make leather. He would soak animal hides (skins) in a special chemical that turned them into leather.

tick— Today, we would call ticks "mattresses." They were stuffed with straw or corn shucks. In the winter, if a family had saved enough feathers, they could also stuff a tick with those.

tradesmen—Tradesmen were men who made things. They were the blacksmiths, carpenters, cobblers (shoemakers), hatters (makers of hats), saddlers (makers of saddles), weavers, etc.

wood box— Chopped wood was stored inside in a wood box to be kept dry. Wood boxes would stand nearby the stove or fireplace where their wood was needed.